OSD

Egyptian Stories

Retold by Robert Hull
Illustrated by Barbara Loftus
and Noël Bateman

Wayland

Tales From Around The World

African Stories
British Stories
Egyptian Stories
Greek Stories
Native North American Stories
Norse Stories
Roman Stories

Editor: Katie Roden
Series Designer: Tracy Gross
Book Designer: Mark Whitchurch
Colour illustrations by Barbara Loftus
Black and white artwork by Noël Bateman
Map on page 47 by Peter Bull
Consultant: Dr Richard Parkinson, Curator,
Department of Egyptian Antiquities,
British Museum, London

First published in 1993 by
Wayland (Publishers) Ltd
61 Western Road, Hove
East Sussex BN3 1JD, England

British Library Cataloguing in Publication Data

Hull, Robert
Egyptian Stories. – (Tales from Around
the World Series)
I. Title II. Series
398.20932

ISBN 0-7502-0832-5

Typeset by Dorchester Typesetting Group Ltd
Printed in Italy by G. Canale & C.S.p.A., Turin

Contents

Introduction

Words must have been important to the ancient Egyptians. In one story the god Ptah makes the world by speaking the names of things. As he speaks, they come into being.

King Shabaka of Nubia found this creation story on a papyrus roll when he invaded Memphis in the seventh century BC. Papyrus was a kind of paper made from reeds, and it crumbled easily. To make sure the story was never lost, King Shabaka ordered it to be carved on a stone. In that way it was saved for us to read, even though the stone was eventually used as a millstone, and much of the writing was worn off.

The Egyptians wrote in hieroglyphs, which are beautifully designed drawings of objects like the sun, a falcon, a baboon and so on. At first each hieroglyph stood for the object in the carving, but as time went on hieroglyphs represented sounds as well. The Egyptians painted or carved stories, prayers and spells on the walls of tombs, on coffins, on statues, and on ordinary household objects. For instance, one inscription has been found on a box of eye make-up.

Because the Egyptians wrote so much and for such a long time, stories have been saved from even three or four thousand years ago. Many are stories of how the world began – creation stories. Different parts of ancient Egypt had different beliefs. In one region the first gods were all frog-headed and the first goddesses had serpent heads. In another the first being was a great fish that turned into a cow.

4

But there was at least one thing that all Egyptians believed in, and that was the River Nile. Nearly every year, between July and October, the Nile filled up with swirling flood waters that were used to water the fields and make crops grow. Nearly every year, they brought Egypt to life, but sometimes the flood failed, and there was hunger and perhaps famine.

So the real 'Egypt' is a thin ribbon of farmed land, with empty deserts on each side. In the stories, the desert is Seth, the god of destruction, with his fierce winds; the Nile in flood is the god Osiris, renewing life.

But not all Egyptian stories are serious, to do with matters of creation or the struggle between life and death. There are magical and fantastic stories. There are stories that poke fun at the kings of Egypt, the Pharaohs. There are comic stories and animal stories. You will find all those kinds of story here.

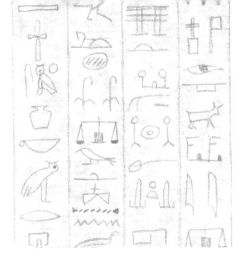

The First Light

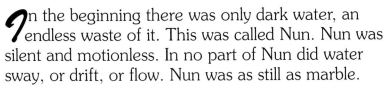

In the beginning there was only dark water, an endless waste of it. This was called Nun. Nun was silent and motionless. In no part of Nun did water sway, or drift, or flow. Nun was as still as marble.

For many aeons of time, in the watery blackness of Nun, nothing moved.

Then, after countless ages of stillness, there was a movement.

It was a grain of mud, shifting against another grain. One of the grains was loosened and swayed freely upwards through the darkness. That first movement started others, and grain after grain of mud rose to the top of the waters and gathered there with the others. In time they became a small mud bank. This was the First Mound of the world. This was the First Place.

Then the First Lotus came to the First Place of mud, and opened its blue petals. The darkness became blue, and lightened. From the heart of the First Lotus came the First Light. The First Light was the flushed skin of a child sun-god. The god was called Atum.

Atum grew from the gold centre of the Lotus. The First Light, Atum, shone above the small island of mud, throwing the first rays of light across the waters.

This was the dawn of the first day. After a time the First Lotus closed its petals and went beneath the surface of the waters, drawing Atum down into the depths again, into the darkness of Nun. This was night, when Atum returned to Nun.

The First Gods

*A*tum had been hidden in Nun till he rose from the Lotus.

Atum wanted to make a world. He needed other gods to help him. He made the sound 'Shshshshsh' for a long wilderness of time. He blew continuously above Nun until the empty stillness stirred with the flow and movement of his breath. He had created the god Shu, the air that is made from the hurry of winds round the world.

Next he made the sound 'Tf-tf-tf-tf-tf-tf', spitting it out over and over again for many ages, until the air and the winds were no longer dry but carried in them the moisture of his mouth. He had made moisture and dew, he had made the goddess Tefnut.

The god Shu, air and wind, and the goddess Tefnut, moisture and dew, were always drawn close to each other. From their attraction came two children, a god called Geb and a goddess called Nut.

Geb was the name of the earth and Nut was the name of the sky, and at first they too were so close to each other that they were not really separate. Both Geb and Nut found each other beautiful, and they lay together, sky clinging to earth and earth to sky, so that there was no space between them.

Atum wanted to make the world, and he needed room for things to be. He ordered Shu, the father of Geb and Nut, to separate them and push the sky up away from the earth, so that there would be room for the trees and mountains and other things he wanted to make.

Shu crawled in between Geb and Nut, and forced himself to his feet. He levered Nut upwards, as if he were pushing up a heavy tent. He held Geb down, and while Geb struggled under Shu's feet, making the first earthquakes, Shu pushed Nut's body higher and higher till it made the shape of an arch above Geb. Finally Geb, the earth, lay still, and Nut, the sky, curved in a silent arch high above him, and Shu stood holding up Nut, holding her away from Geb. And since then the earth has been parted from the sky.

Atum took pity on Geb, separated from his wife. So that Geb could still see Nut clearly, Atum made thousands of stars, and scattered them out along her body. Shu had to hold it all in place. Sometimes he tires of holding up the arching body of Nut, with the extra weight of the stars, and then Nut leans nearer to earth, showing her old love for Geb. That is what is happening on those nights when men and women say the stars seem especially clear and close.

In the gap Shu made by lifting up the sky, Atum was able to make things and give them space to grow. He brought into being mountains, rivers, deserts, animals, trees and plants. He asked Tefnut, the moisture goddess, to carry her mists, dews and damp winds amongst the new trees and plants. She did, and a thousand colours and scents soon came from them, in gratitude for being made.

All these new things made by Atum seemed to want to surge up from the earth. Plants grew straight upwards, men and women lifted themselves higher up on two legs, mountains reached through the clouds. At dawn the scents of the lotus and the sycamore wavered and drifted up into the blue, at evening the smoke from fires headed straight for the stars. Geb, the earth, still expressed his yearning for Nut,

for his old love the dazzling blue sky, who arched forever out of his reach.

All this Atum had made. He had forced himself out of the blackness of Nun and risen from the First Lotus. Then he had made the first gods, Shu and Tefnut, the gods of wind and air and moisture. In turn they had made Geb, the earth, and Nut, the sky.

At last, after aeons of time, a small gap had been made in the blackness. An opening had been made in Nun, a cave of light in the great darkness. But Nun, the watery blackness, still surrounded everything. Nun went under the new world and all around it, threatening to break back into it.

The gods had work to do. They had to make sure that the black waters did not crash back into the small world and wash it away to nothing.

10

The Children of Sky and Earth

*N*ut, the sky, had loved Geb, the earth, and she was pregnant.

Atum feared this. In the space that Shu kept clear between Nut and Geb, Atum had already built mountains and valleys and drawn rivers from the rocks; he had spread out forests and deserts and had carved animals and distributed them to run there. He had created other gods to help him: gods of the moon, of knowledge, of flood. But Atum still had work to do and he feared that Nut might want to return to be with Geb, her old lover, the father of her children-to-be. If she did there would be no space for Atum to arrange the rest of his creation. There would not be a large enough clearing in the darkness of Nun. Its waters might return and flood through the new world.

Atum decided that Nut could not have her children in the world. She could not give birth to them during any of the days or nights of the world.

The days of the world were three hundred and sixty. That was the number of times Atum ended the day and went below the earth, descending into the waters of Nun near the Mountains of the Evening. Three hundred and sixty times, at the end of the day, Atum journeyed beneath the earth, through the waters of Nun, before he rose again near the Mountains of the Dawn. Three hundred and sixty times Atum made his journey over and under the earth, each one on a different path, visiting the whole world.

11

The god Thoth took pity on Nut. Thoth was the wisest of the gods whom Atum had created. When Thoth found out that Atum had banned Nut from having her children during the world's days, he thought deeply. He needed time – enough time to make more days and give them to Nut.

Thinking, he scratched with flint on stone. He drew a design of circles on a round, white stone. He carved the same design on a dark stone.

Thoth moved the light stone over the dark one; it was like Atum, the sun, going high above Nun. When Atum travelled above Nun there was no darkness; it was as if Nun had gone. It gave Thoth an idea. He carried the light stone over the dark stone again, and hid the dark stone behind him, out of sight. The light stone had taken the dark away. There could be a game with suns and darknesses, a game of many worlds.

Thoth invented the game of draughts from his thinking. He would play it with Moon, the god who measured time. He would win time for Nut. Thoth carved circles on many light and dark stones and showed them to the other gods. When he explained the game, they wanted to play.

Thoth played against Moon, and won. He played again, and won.

Many times they played, and many times Thoth won. Moon had to give some of his time to Thoth. Thoth won five days of time in all, and gave them to the beautiful Nut to have her children in. From that time on, Moon lacked light and was only able to shine at his strongest for a few days each month.

So Nut had her children in time. There were five of them, one for each of the days Thoth had won. Osiris was born on the first day, and then his brothers, Haroeris and Seth, on the next two days. Isis and Nephthys, Nut's daughters, were born on the fourth and fifth days. Now, thanks to Thoth, there were three hundred and sixty-five days in the world.

The Murder of Osiris

$\mathcal{M}$any ages later, when Atum's strength began to fail, Osiris became the greatest of gods. It had been prophesied when he was born. Voices were heard. A woman said that when she was drawing water, she heard a voice echoing in the well-waters: 'Osiris is here, Osiris is here.' At the edge of Nile, men winding in their fishing-nets heard waves saying, 'It is Osiris, it is Osiris.'

In this way Geb had realized that of all his children, his first son, Osiris, would be the strongest in the struggle between the world and the surrounding darkness of Nun. Geb loved Osiris for his determined, peaceful ways, and feared Seth, the younger brother of Osiris. Seth was wild and hot-headed, and loved to run riot and destroy things.

Geb was thinking of ways to bring order into the world, so he decided that when Osiris grew up, he would take over Geb's power. Geb invented the name 'king', and said that to be 'king' would give power. He would give that power to Osiris, he said. Isis would be 'queen', and wife of Osiris. Seth became jealous and angry. He went off into the desert and disappeared.

In time Osiris inherited the world and became god-king. Geb gave him power over the waters, winds, moon and stars. Osiris spoke divine words of power, and his words laid down tracks in the sky for the stars and winds to follow. He carved out paths along the earth to guide the restless waters. He gave the animals

their lengths of time for staying in the world and decided where they should live – the crocodile in water, the baboon in trees, the lion in the desert. He arranged all the world. The wise god Thoth wrote the arrangements down in his book, the Book of Thoth, so that they would never be forgotten.

Because Osiris had given the world regularity and order, people began to understand it. They knew that though every shining moon would thin and die, it would rise again after a few days – if it had not been drowned in the waters of Nun – and grow again above them, bright as silver. When the star Sirius rose in the south they knew that Nile, if it had not died forever, would return and cover the earth like a glittering cloak.

Osiris taught the people of the world when to expect the gentle wind from the north. He taught them how to make buildings and raise them up towards the stars, how to make words, how to write down memories with marks on stone, how to make laws. Osiris spoke a law to stop people killing and eating each other.

Osiris wondered what else he could give to the people. One day, he was walking near Nile, amongst the high barley grasses. A breeze swept through the grass, and Osiris watched the ripe grains being blown through the air and rolling along the earth. Then his sharp eyes noticed that though most of the ripe grains blew away in the wind, some of the heavier ones fell alongside the plant, and stayed there, undisturbed. 'Next year,' he thought, 'those seeds will grow again here, in the same place. Most grains will be scattered and lost, but if a few fall where they have grown, men can gather the grains and keep them. In that way men can make barley grow always in the same place.'

Osiris kept the grain that hadn't blown away, and buried it in the earth. Next year, in the same place, the barley grass grew. He had found the way to make barley stay in one place. He told men to scrape at the earth with sticks and make a safe place to put the heavy barley grain, the grain that fell where it had grown.

Osiris had given the people fields.

Then Osiris saw something else. When Nile came, and the soft wind blew from the north and the world

shone with water, the barley grew more thickly. He told
men and women to dig small channels to the fields and
guide the waters out along these channels. So, with the
guidance of the great god-king Osiris, the people
learned to lead the waters to the barley and spread the
waters there.

Gradually the people had learned to till and sow the
earth and guide water to it from Nile, and to gather the
crops that grew from the fields. Osiris had taught them
to be farmers. He had given them the harvest.

After all this work, Osiris went away from Egypt. He
went to teach these things to other peoples in the east.

Seth, the brother of Osiris, watching from a distance,
had grown even more jealous of his brother's great
power. He had become the opposite of Osiris. He
disliked peace and order. He enjoyed the thrill of
destruction, war and trouble. He loved earthquakes and
storms. His home was the desert and the moonless
night. He fought with his lions and crocodiles on the
side of murder and destruction. It was easy for him to
decide that he wanted to destroy everything Osiris had
made.

Seth planned a terrible death for his brother. When
Osiris returned from his travels, Seth invited him to a
feast. Seth had made a beautiful chest, with a sky of
stars painted under the lid. He pretended that he
wanted to find out which guest would be the right size
for it. Knowing all along that it was exactly the right
size for Osiris, he persuaded all the guests to lie in it
one after the other.

It was a compliment to his guests that Seth was
offering such a gift to them, and they all tried the chest
with pleasure. None of them fitted. When Osiris lay in
it, fitting perfectly, Seth and his accomplices
immediately hammered the lid shut and poured molten
lead into the cracks to prevent Osiris from breathing.
Then they took the chest, with Osiris inside, and hurled
it into Nile.

Osiris lay dying inside his chest as it floated on Nile
and then out beyond Nile into a great sea. It drifted for
many days and finally came to rest in the shade of a
sycamore tree, at a place called Byblos. Soon, the
sycamore began to grow. Quickly it mounted and

spread to a huge size, its massive trunk thickening round the casket of Osiris, hiding it as if in another chest.

When the king of Byblos was told about the huge, fast-growing tree at the sea-shore, he had it cut down. Not knowing that Osiris was trapped inside it, he used the trunk as the main pillar of his palace hall. Osiris was not only unburied, but lost. No one knew where his body was.

After Osiris died, Nile died. The land along Nile died too. Instead of sharing the glittering joy of living Nile, the world seemed lifeless. It was all waste and desert, scoured by hot winds that wanted to scavenge and destroy. There was no energy in the world, flowers and grass were burnt, animals grew listless.

Men and women were afraid of the death of Nile. Now they knew that Osiris was gone, the people feared that Nile might never again send small streams whispering messages along the ditches and dikes to tell the waiting barley to begin to grow.

Osiris had taught men and women to make places where they could speak to Nile and give thanks to it when it came. Now they tried to speak: 'Canal of happiness, come again. Flood the fields with plenty. Rise again, spill us your waters in happiness, keep the world bathed in shimmering life . . . ' But the words failed, the people were without belief. The power of Osiris was gone from their words.

Throughout all this grieving time, Isis, the sister and wife of the dead Osiris, had been looking for him. Keeping her young child, Horus, safely with her, she wandered through the places where Nile had lived, and asked everyone she met if anyone had seen the chest of Osiris. No one had. On and on she went, and came to the place where Nile, when it was living, had divided and spread into lesser Niles that wandered amongst islands and marshes. Some children told her that when Nile was there they had seen a painted box float by them, to join the Great Green Water to the north.

Isis had to follow the body of Osiris, even though it meant leaving Horus. 'Guard him well,' she said to the cobra-goddess Wadjet, who said she would gladly look after him.

18

'I will guard him, Isis. We shall go to the floating island called Chemmis. Only the quiet sea winds and the scent of the waters can reach us there.'

Isis was satisfied. Letting the wind take her along the coast the way Osiris would have drifted, Isis sailed for days, and finally let her boat drift ashore near the mouth of a river. She saw some children playing at the edge of the sea, and some young women washing clothes and swimming. Isis asked them if they had seen the chest. None of them had.

Isis looked round her, scanning the beach. She must carry on searching, but for some reason she could not easily leave these women and their children. Then her eyes met the sad, large-eyed gaze of a thin, wasted young boy.

'Who are you, my child?' the goddess asked.

'I am the king's son.'

'You are very thin for a king's son.'

'I cannot eat.'

Isis wasn't only a goddess, she was a mother, and she felt a rush of motherly pity. For the moment, she almost forgot her husband Osiris, and even her little son Horus, in a sudden new anxiety for a stranger, a dying child.

'I can heal him,' she said to the young women, and so they asked her to go with them. After a few minutes' walk, with the king's son leading the way, Isis found herself face to face with the king and queen of Byblos. 'I can perform the cure this very night, if you will let me do it in my own way.'

'We have no other hope,' the king said.

Isis did not know she was near to finding the chest of Osiris. But that night she discovered it.

She had decided not just to heal the king's son, but to make him a god, an immortal. She pitied him, and his peaceful, quiet ways reminded her of Osiris. To make the boy immortal she had to burn away his mortal self, the part that would fade and decay, the part that had fallen ill.

For the ceremony Isis turned herself into a swallow. Next she made a fire, the fire of her love, and fanned it with her swallow's wings. Fainting in its flames, his heart rushing and being reborn in the trembling wind

of her wings, the young boy was on the edge of being taken into immortality. Isis was filling his nostrils and mouth with sweet-scented goddess breath, when, with a shriek of terror, the queen ran from behind the pillar. She had been watching; the ceremony terrified her. She broke into the magic rite and it failed. Her son would die.

From the beak of Isis broke a thin cry of despair. She flew wildly round and round, fluttering above the boy and beating her wings hopelessly. Finally, her heart racing, she flew to rest against the upright pillar. In that instant she felt the dimmed power of Osiris, buried deep in the dead wood, signalling weakly up to her.

Isis had found her dead husband. In a few minutes the king's workmen opened the pillar and hewed out the chest. The king gave it to Isis. She put the body of Osiris in her boat and began the journey back to Egypt.

Seth was waiting. He was camped, with all his cruel accomplices, in the marshes. When Isis stopped to rest, on a night when the moon-eye of Thoth was wide open, pouring its silver gaze into the reeds and water, Seth saw the gleam of the chest he had painted. He broke it open, took the body of Osiris, carved it into pieces, and gave them to his accomplices; he ordered them to journey with the bits of Osiris' body to the ends of Egypt and hide them. Then Osiris could never be reborn; his power would be broken. The world would be as Seth wanted it, dead and burnt, like a desert. Nile, the bringer of life, would never come again.

For a second time, Isis had lost Osiris. She could neither bury him properly nor try to bring him to life again. Then, to add to her grief, her small son Horus fell dangerously ill, bitten by a scorpion.

The new griefs of Isis seemed to give her renewed strength. Instead of paralysing her they drove her on. Leaving her sick son in the care of Wadjet, she started out again to find the scattered remains of Osiris.

In her swallow shape, Isis headed into the burning winds, along the dry remains of Nile, searching, swooping low under the shrivelled trees at its edge. Soon she thought she felt the flickering pulse of Osiris' being nearby. She swerved round and went hurtling back along the bank, then sheered away over the reeds, twittering with grief.

He was near. She felt him. There was a faint trembling from his presence. She alighted on a rope where a boat was tied up. A few feet away, she saw an arm of Osiris, half-buried in the sand.

On the bank Isis made a small altar of stones and wood. It would mark the spot, and be a temple.

Then on she went, driving her wings along the length of empty Nile. Grief gave her the energy to scour through every grove of palms and dart in and out of every boatyard and farmhouse. In time Isis discovered all the places where Seth's henchmen had thrown the remains of Osiris: a small cave, a ruined shepherd's hut, a dried-up canal. Wherever she found a piece of him, she built a small temple. Through the power of her grief, she began to defeat Seth. In a bitter harvest, she gathered in the whole body of Osiris.

In secret, in a cool tomb under the ground at the edge of Nile, Isis pieced together her husband's body and bound it in white cloth. She bent over it as she had bent over the young child in Byblos. She breathed her goddess-scented breath into his mouth and nostrils. She beat her wings over him. His broken body had gone from the light above into the cool kingdom under the earth, but his sleeping spirit could still waken. It could still live as king in the underworld and could still bring life to the world above.

With the passionate beating of Isis' wings came the first sign. The burning winds from the south died, and a

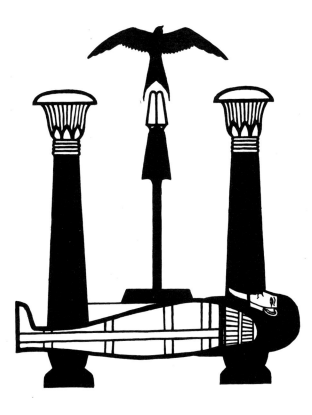

cool, lemon-scented breeze sprang up from the north. The spirit of Osiris was waking. Then, slowly, Nile's wasted, thin waters rose, spread themselves, and returned to the places they had neglected. Nile was waking. The waters glinted, greeting the new wind. Beneath its blustery strength they waved their white flags, honouring Osiris.

Horus, the sick son of Isis and Osiris, hidden far away on the floating island, in the same moment began to recover, as Isis beat her wings above Osiris. Seeing the spirit of Osiris stir, she wound her way up through the dark tomb and out into the light, on her way towards Horus.

She flew high over Nile. She saw how Nile, blue with the reflected sky, was reaching its arms gladly into the land. She swooped lower. She saw how its white waters tumbled down steps, overflowed dikes, went flouncing down the narrow mud-alleys. The dikes throbbed white, the flat canals gleamed. Egypt shone.

As Isis flew overhead, she saw the first green shoots come up, like spirits released from the darkness under the earth. Osiris lived.

So Isis returned to her healed son, Horus. She told him he would need to help the spirit of his father. Horus had to watch the fields and protect them. He had to look after the people who tilled the fields and gathered the harvest. Soon Horus would have to rise into the sky as a falcon and search the world with his fierce gaze to make sure that it stayed as Osiris had made it. He would have to guard the land against Seth, who wanted to take it and be the next king.

And so Osiris lived, but not as he had before. In his under-kingdom he ruled the spirits of all the dead, and returned each year to give life to Nile and to the land of Nile.

Stealing the Book of Thoth

*W*ho'd be a farmer? Seth sends terrible dry winds, the gods hold the flood back so you've not enough water, officials swipe half your crop for the Pharaoh. Not to mention the hippo charging in for a free feed of corn, alongside the hungry rats and pigeons. No, I'd sooner be a scribe. Your own boss, no taxes, you stay inside in the cool when you want to. And you get some respect. As the wise man said, 'Good words are more precious than ivory.' They don't say that about a good crop of onions, do they?

I'm not brilliant at scribing. I can write hieroglyphs on papyrus, but I can't carve them very well. Otherwise I'm an ordinary person, an ordinary scribe, and I'm happy enough. The trouble with writing is that it can go to your head. You think you're a god like Ptah, making things real just because you write them down. Then you want the secrets of more and more words. It can lead to disaster. I'll tell you how. It was in a story I read, on a papyrus scroll.

There was a scribe who had a thirst to know everything. His name was Setna. He was the king's son. His father had made him priest of the temple of Ptah at Memphis, and he spent all his time studying writings and copying them, and perfecting spells and charms. He neglected his wife and children, all because of his ambition to become a great magician. Even when he was still a young man, he'd copied out the entire Library of Magical Scrolls.

One day Setna was reading some inscriptions in the temple of Ptah when an old priest stopped to talk to him. The priest had always tried to study, but was ending his life with only a little knowledge, and had become very jealous of the king's clever son. He decided to throw some temptation in his way.

'My lord, would you like to learn much more? Would you like to have a thousand times more knowledge than you have now?'

'I seek to learn everything,' Setna replied.

'These inscriptions give you only a little power. I can tell you where the greatest power lies.'

'Where?'

'In the Book of Thoth. In his great book the god of knowledge has written down everything that is known. In his book are recorded the true number of the stars, and their journeys. The instructions to rivers and winds are written there. Some pages are written in the languages of birds, others in the words of animals. If you know the spells written in the Book of Thoth you can command the stars, control the winds and waterfalls, and communicate with all creatures.'

Setna could hardly believe what he was hearing. To look into the Book of Thoth, the book of all the knowledge in the world! What power there would be in that book! He wanted that power. 'Where? Where is this great and fabulous book?'

'In the tomb of Neferkaptah. The Book of Thoth lies there, in a chamber deep under the earth, a chamber lit by the eternal radiance of the book.'

Setna went straight to his father, King Ramesses.

'Father, I have a request. I wish to be allowed to enter the tomb of Neferkaptah and gaze on the Book of Thoth. I wish to open it and see its words. One page will quench my raging thirst for its knowledge, father.'

Fearing Setna's great need for knowledge and power, Ramesses was reluctant to give permission, but he knew that the Kas, the visible spirits of the dead who lived in the tombs with their owners, would guard the book. He finally said Setna could enter the tomb.

Only a brave man, or someone as determined as Setna, would go deep under the earth and walk the dark streets of the City of the Dead. Even the workmen were afraid, when they were ordered to find the wooden outer door of the tomb. But they found where it lay hidden in the sand, and unsealed it. Then they hurried away.

There were steps. Setna lit a torch, and down he went, from the sun's burning heat into the cool, musty dark. As he went deeper it became warmer. Then the steps ended and a corridor began. It went on and on, bending first one way, then another.

Ahead of him he saw daylight. How could that be? He had been travelling downhill all this time. As he went forward the light grew stronger. Then Setna remembered the words of the priest: 'The eternal radiance of the book.'

One last bend in the corridor, and Setna found himself in an open chamber flooded with light. The light was not coming in from outside, or through gaps in the roof or chinks in the rock. It was radiating from the altar in the centre of the chamber. It came from the object that lay on the altar – the Book of Thoth. The book threw the light of a thousand torches along every corridor that led to the chamber, so that Setna did not at first see the quietly glowing Kas of Anhur, wife of Neferkaptah, and of her son Merab.

Setna went round the chamber. It was just like a room in a palace, he thought. He sat on one of the ebony chairs, then on the couch. He went across to the table, and picked up one of the fruit bowls. There were drinking vessels. There was a set of draughts and even a beer sieve – so beer was gritty even after death! – and a small ivory make-up tray. Setna was so fascinated that he almost forgot why he had come. Then he turned towards the light of the book.

'Why have you come here?'

The voice from behind chilled him to the bones. He turned to see the glowing Ka of Anhur. She spoke again. 'Why have you come?'

Setna realized that the beautiful woman-figure, glowing like the reflection of a lotus in the water, was a Ka, a ghost person. The spirit of Anhur was here in the tomb with her husband's body, but her body itself was not here. Something was wrong; Kas usually stayed with their owner's body.

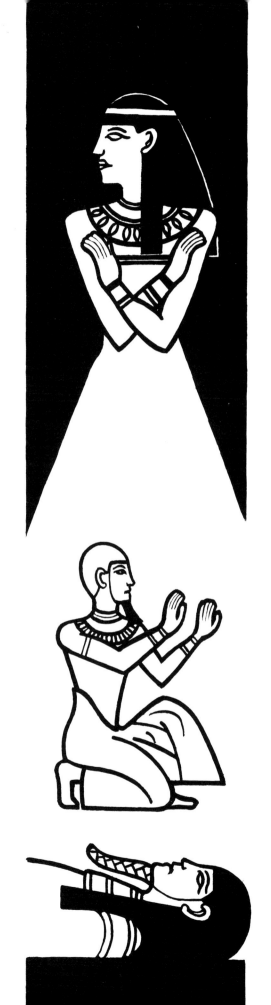

Setna replied, 'I am a scholar and magician. With the permission of my father, Ramesses, I have come to read the Book of Thoth.' Setna was already in the grip of his desires. He had said to his father that he wished to read one page. Now he spoke of 'reading the book'.

Anhur spoke again. 'Do not ever seek to read the Book of Thoth. Go back the way you have come before any harm comes to you, as harm came to me, my son and my husband. I shall tell you a story, to warn you. Sit with us.' She pushed an ebony chair forward, and Setna sat and looked at her gently glowing face.

'My husband's body, wrapped in white linen, lies before you on the golden couch. His is the masked head that reclines on the alabaster head-rest. It is because of the Book of Thoth that he lies there. It is because of the Book of Thoth that he and I and my son Merab no longer live together in the bright air as man, woman and boy.

'My husband was like you. He longed to know everything. He too spent many bright days in the long dusk of libraries and temples, studying sacred sentences and learning deep inscriptions. One day a priest came up to him and told him that such slight words were of little use to him. It would take Neferkaptah all his life, the priest said, to gather even a few grains of sand from the beaches of knowledge. Neferkaptah would never quench his great thirst, the priest said, unless he acquired the Book of Thoth. Then the priest told him where it was.'

'Was it not always here?' Setna asked.

'Ah no, Setna, it was at the bottom of a deep river.'

'At the bottom of a river?!' Setna was astonished.

'The priest said to my husband Neferkaptah, "The Book of Thoth is hidden deep in a river, far to the south, near Coptos. It is bound in an iron casket. It is surrounded by living chains of writhing, unkillable water serpents. Inside the iron casket is a second casket of copper, inside the copper casket another one of juniper wood, then one of ebony and one of ivory, then one of silver, then one of gold. The Book of Thoth lies in the innermost casket, the seventh. But you will never be able to defeat the serpents."

'Neferkaptah could not resist. I begged him not to go but he would not listen. He took us with him and we sailed to Coptos in a boat that the king lent us. At Coptos, Neferkaptah left Merab and myself with the priests of the temple of Isis, while he sailed on. When he came back a few days later he told us what had happened. He had come to the place where the box lay in the depths of the river, and there he had spoken a great river-spell, which made the water recoil on each side of the boat. There gleamed the metal box, smeared with mud, a tangle of serpents clustered round it.

'Neferkaptah took a sword to the hissing serpents, and at first their heads grew back every time he hacked one off. But when he threw sand between the severed halves, they could not join up to grow another head. The snakes lost their grip, and went swirling away into the current. One by one he hacked the boxes open, and finally, there it was, the radiant Book of Thoth, in the seventh box.

'Neferkaptah stole the book from the river. He took it back to the palace and began studying the long scrolls. In a short time he learned the languages of the ibis, the hoopoe and the vulture. He learned the words of the crocodile and the baboon. He began to enchant the winds and direct the uncertain waters. He showed some of the scroll to me. Together we copied spells, crumbling the fresh papyrus in beer and swallowing the incantations, so that their power would always be part of us.

'We became powerful. But Thoth is more powerful, and is a god. He told the other gods that Neferkaptah had insulted the river and taken the Book of Thoth, with all the world's knowledge in it. The gods gave Thoth permission to take revenge. It was swift, unexpected and merciless. As we were sailing back from Coptos, my husband and I were dozing under an awning in the noon heat, when little Merab, who was playing on deck, fell over the side and was drowned.

29

'No spell could bring Merab back. No spell could lighten my dark grief. Many months later, passing the same place, I drank much beer to forget, and with the help of Thoth – for so I believe – I too fell to my death. My body was taken to Coptos, to be with the body of Merab.

'Sailing back to Memphis, Neferkaptah realized that he could not bear life without us. Wrapping himself round with strips of linen that made it impossible to swim, he bound the Book of Thoth to his side, then hurled himself over the stern of the boat. The crew searched the river for him but found nothing, and so they sailed on. When they arrived at Memphis his body was found tangled in the steering ropes, with the book.

'The priests of Thoth said that it was an omen; the book should be buried with him because it caused his death. So he was buried here, near Memphis, and the Book of Thoth was buried in the tomb with him. I came here with the Ka of Merab to be with him, though our two bodies are far away, in Coptos.

'So you can see, Setna, how a fierce greed for knowledge led to terrible things. My husband's theft killed us all. Do not steal the Book of Thoth, Setna, do not risk a terrible fate.'

Kas cannot weep, but the strange, thin voice of the Ka of Anhur, drifting from her slow-moving, glimmering mouth, was full of desperate regret. And yet, though Setna had heard all her appalling story, he was not frightened. The drownings had happened to others, to the gloomy dead. He could be much more careful. He would hide, and learn from the book the most secret places of the world. He realized at the very same moment that like Neferkaptah, he would take the book, not just read it as he had intended.

Setna went slowly forward towards the book. 'Your deaths are the past. The book is my future.'

He was just about to lay hands on it when a hollow, stifled voice came from behind the mask of Neferkaptah, like a voice coiling up from a dry well. 'No. No.' The body was moving. Setna went cold, then he could only watch, stiff with fear, as if he were half mummy himself, while the body slowly, slowly, turned onto its side. One arm edged forward and pushed

down, levering the body upward till the mummy of
Neferkaptah was leaning on one elbow.

'No,' the voice came again. 'Not theft. Not taking by
force. Play. Play for the book with Thoth's counters.
Four games of draughts, one for each of us here. If you
lose, the earth can wrap itself round you. If you win,
you can fasten the Book of Thoth to your side and rise
into the air. If you take it with skill, Thoth may forgive.
Or not. But not if you take it by theft.'

The figure sank back down. The Ka of Anhur
brought the draughts from the table, and Setna played
against the body of Neferkaptah, waiting even longer
than players do in life for his opponent to decide each
move then to carry the pieces slowly over the board.
Not only were Neferkaptah's hands and arms unused
to movement, his brain had stiffened and could hardly
remember how to play.

But Neferkaptah had once studied the secret
patterns of draughts in the Book of Thoth, just as he
had learned the journeys of the stars. None of them
could be forgotten. He played, and won. The earth
folded itself round the ankles of Setna. A second game.
Neferkaptah won, and the earth swathed Setna up to
the waist. A third. Setna was buried up to the lips.

The fourth game began. Setna started to lose pieces.
Then he remembered one of the great spells he had
learned in the Library of Magical Scrolls. It was a spell
for weakening the dark powers of night. He tried it
now on the black pieces of Neferkaptah, speaking it
over and over.

Neferkaptah had not sufficient memory to summon
words to stop the march of the white pieces, and Setna
won the fateful fourth game. He shouted with triumph,
swept the rest of the pieces from the table, snatched
the Book of Thoth, and ran from the chamber.

Along the winding corridors of the tomb ran Setna,
out into the bright air. He went straight to his father's
palace. He told Ramesses that he had found and taken
the Book of Thoth. Ramesses was fearful for him.

'Setna, it is better that you do not possess the book.
Thoth himself, and the rest of the gods, will punish
you. They will humiliate you for your pride. They will
make you ignorant for wanting too much knowledge.'

'Father, with the book I can do anything and become anything. No god can make me ignorant again. No god will find me when I am a small bird, or a grain of sand at the edge of Nile. I have the gods' knowledge. I am more powerful than they.'

Setna could not be persuaded to give up the book. He went straight to his room and unrolled it. As he read, secret after secret came flooding into his mind. He practised incantations. The next day he went to the edge of Nile and at his summons hippos came trundling up to him. On the second day he heard what the ibis said. On the third day he pulled Nile under a sandy bluff and toppled the bluff into the water. On the fourth day he intended to make the moon shine brighter.

But it was on the fourth day that the gods struck.

Instead of a brighter moon, a moon that would come nearer to him, Setna saw, as he walked the crowded streets, a woman with a beautiful face that shone like the moon. She came close by him, and for a moment her eyes caught his. Setna had never seen a woman he so much wanted to speak to. His sudden need for her was like his mad desire for the Book of Thoth. He turned to watch her pass along the street, and then she was gone.

Setna sent his servant after her to find out who she was. In a short while the servant came back with the news that her name was Tabube, and that she was the daughter of a priest who was visiting the temple of Ptah. Her home was in the north, at Bubastis, the servant said, and Tabube and her father had already gone on board a boat ready to leave.

For the rest of that day Setna could think of nothing but Tabube. The next morning, forgetting his family and the Book of Thoth, he took a boat for Bubastis.

He arrived the following day, and found Tabube's house. He went in and asked to speak to her. Setna said he was a prince who had discovered great power, and that when he had seen Tabube in Memphis near the temple of Ptah, he had immediately wished to share his power with her.

Tabube sent her servant to tell Setna to come to her. She was waiting for him in her chamber, lying on a

couch. On a table next to her were dishes of pomegranates and figs, and two glasses of red wine.

'Why have you come?' asked Tabube.

'I have fallen in love with you,' Setna said. 'I wish to be with you. All I have is yours.'

'Sit near me, Setna,' she said. 'Let us drink.'

Setna should have wondered why she welcomed him, a stranger, so warmly. He should have been puzzled that she knew his name. But he was drunk before he touched a drop of her wine, drunk with fascination. He knew nothing of what was happening, and didn't try to understand. He had been made ignorant.

But Tabube knew very well what she was doing. Thoth had told her that she would be able to enchant Setna in the simplest way, not with magic but with her long, shining, black hair, her grey eyes, her voice.

She let him kiss her. And again. 'If you wish to marry me,' she said, 'there must be a contract of agreement.' Setna nodded. Tabube summoned a slave, who presented Setna with a papyrus roll. 'Read this,' Tabube said. Setna did. The contract said that when Setna married Tabube, all he had would be hers just as he had said.

Setna signed it. With a few strokes of a writing brush, and without thinking what he was doing, he promised that Tabube would have his house, his wealth, even his wife and his children. If he had Tabube, everything she possessed would also be his. And though he was already married, his first wife was far away.

'Let us drink to our agreement,' said Tabube, with a smile. They both drank. Tabube laughed quietly. 'Now the story is nearly over,' she said. Setna smiled too, not knowing what she meant, but feeling happier than he had ever felt. He leaned towards her, his arms reaching out, his eyes closed, to embrace her.

He toppled over into the dust. His arms stretched along the ground, his face touched the path. People were stepping round him, making comments: 'A madman'; 'He must be drunk.'

Setna looked around him. He was surrounded by ordinary streets and people. It was a dull, unreal world.

Someone had stolen the real, radiant world. Tabube's house was nowhere to be seen. The walled garden, her chamber, her shining hair, the marriage contract – gone, as if they had never existed.

He walked in a daze along the street. Slowly he began to think. Perhaps that radiant, vanished world was not real? Perhaps his other life, his life at Memphis, was the real world. Were his wife and children still there, in his house in Memphis? He had to hurry back to find out.

On the way back to Memphis Setna thought deeply. Some of his knowledge returned to him. He knew that if he wanted back his real life in Memphis he had to restore the Book of Thoth to the chamber of Neferkaptah.

Ramesses was glad to see his son again, and even more pleased that he intended to return the Book of Thoth. Setna was overjoyed to see that his wife and children were with Ramesses in the palace. While he had been away, his wife told him, their house had been burnt down, and both the children had been terribly ill and nearly died.

Setna knew, somehow, that the lives of his children had been in his hands. Their lives had gone sailing towards the dark and had only turned back towards life and light at the very moment he had decided to restore the book.

The light came back into Setna's life on the same day that the radiance of the Book of Thoth again filled the burial chamber of Neferkaptah.

Setna also saw to it that the bodies of Anhur and Merab were brought to Memphis, so that all the family would be together in the tomb.

King Solomon and the Burning Sun

One day King Solomon was travelling south on his great silk-tasselled square carpet, hauled through the air by four djinns pulling at the corners. It was a burning hot morning, and Solomon wanted protection from the sun. The carpet went through the air quickly, but not fast enough to make a really cooling breeze.

When he saw some vultures sailing along in the opposite direction, he had an idea. He called down to the djinns to stop the carpet and hover for a minute. Solomon knew all the languages of the birds, and he hailed the nearest vulture. 'Vulture, I need your help! I request that you gather your flock above me and protect me from the sun. Fly with me as a shield from the sun and I will reward you handsomely!'

The vultures flapped round in circles for a while, consulting, and then one hopped on to the carpet, ruffling out his thick neck feathers as proudly as any rooster. Then he put his head on one side, rather apologetically, and squawked a few words. 'We would like to help you, King, but unfortunately we are on our way to a sumptuous feast in Memphis. Stuffed pigeon, sorbets, wine, various kinds of beans, dancing girls and so on. I'm sorry we cannot help. But have a good journey.' The vulture gave a little 'grawk' and launched himself over the side, then he and the rest of the vultures flapped off towards the north.

Solomon was furious. The vultures did not seem to realize that he was the chief of the air himself, and had power over them as their king. He cursed the vultures in long, kingly curses. 'Foul birds, my magic merciless revenge decrees that you go bare-necked in the fierce desert sun, bare-necked in the scouring sand-winds, bare-necked in the stone-splitting freezing nights.' That was the end of the thick covering of beautiful feathers along the vultures' long necks. Some storytellers say that the vultures lost them at that very moment, in mid-flight to Memphis, and were too embarrassed to attend the feast there. They say that farmers were amazed to see a rain of black feathers twisting down out of the sky. That may all be an exaggeration, but it is true that from that time on vultures had ugly, long, scraggy, featherless necks, and were ridiculed by more stylish birds.

That was not all. After Solomon had resumed his flight he had another thought, and stopped the carpet again. Then he delivered a second curse. 'Foul birds, I have decided that vultures shall fly to no more fabulous feasts up and down the country. Vultures shall wait till the lion has had his fill, and shall make do on lifeless leftovers. From now on vultures shall be summoned to meals in the dead intestines of camels and the forgotten flesh of baboons. And they shall wait and wait interminably for their foul scraps, circling and circling in the air, or crouching in the dusty shadows.'

Solomon felt much better for his two long curses, but no cooler. Then he saw some hoopoes flying along. He thought how fine they looked in the sun, with their long beaks, orange shoulders and their brilliant black and white wings. They pleased him, as they flicked and floated along, or abruptly changed direction with great skill. He called them over and made the same request as he had to the vultures. The king of the hoopoes alighted on the carpet and said that they were very small birds, and it would be difficult for only a few of them to give much protection, but he would gather as many birds as he could.

And that is what the king of the hoopoes did. A crowd of twittering hoopoes soon gathered, then more, and as more and more birds came, their shadow spread over the whole carpet. Then Solomon started his journey again, with a thousand hoopoes forming an

awning over him. At first, the carpet and the bird-cloud found it difficult to keep flying at exactly the same speed, and when the carpet rose to go over a mountain or dropped down suddenly in a current of air, the carpet slipped from under the edge of the shadow. But the birds were skilful fliers, and Solomon, in the middle of the carpet, made the rest of the journey in cool shade.

Solomon wished to reward the hoopoes, and when they arrived at his palace he asked their king what extra dignity he could give to them for shading him on the journey. The king of the hoopoes was not sure what to say, and he was confused in the surroundings of the palace. So he said, 'Can we fly off a little way and have time to consider your kind offer?'

Solomon agreed, and the hoopoes flew off in a dizzying whirl of black and white.

They settled at the edge of the city to talk things over. It was difficult to decide. Some hoopoes wanted to be much bigger and have short, fierce beaks like eagles. Some wanted to change their wings and instead of black and white bars have red, blue or green. Then one of them said, 'Why don't we ask Solomon for a golden crown on our heads, like his own?'

All the hoopoes thought that was the best idea, and the king flew back to inform Solomon of their decision. At first Solomon said he didn't think it was a very good idea for them to fly round in the open with real gold on their heads, but he agreed to arrange it. After all, he had promised them whatever they requested.

In the workshops of the goldsmiths work began at once, hammering innumerable crests of gold for all the hoopoes. The gold needed to be hammered fine, so as not to drag the birds down in flight or spoil their beautiful acrobatics. But eventually, with advice from Thoth, the god of wisdom, the goldsmiths succeeded in designing a gold crest that would make the hoopoes even more beautiful and yet not alter their flight. Soon all the hoopoes had crests that shone in the sun with the unmistakable glitter of pure gold.

Solomon had been right to worry. In a few weeks the hoopoes had become precious. They were being killed for the gold of their crests. Hundreds of hoopoes died. The kingdom of the hoopoes was troubled. Their numbers dwindled. Finally the few who were left were priceless, and teams of hunters searched relentlessly for their hiding places.

The king of the hoopoes returned to Solomon. 'What can be done?' he asked. Solomon made his suggestion. 'Let all hoopoes give up the pure gold of their crest, but keep a golden crest, made not of metal, but of feathers. Let the feathers of the crest be gold only in colour. The hoopoe's crest will still be a joy to it, and to those who watch it. And the hoopoe will no longer be hunted, and will flourish.'

Solomon was a wise king over the birds. On the hoopoes' heads feathers grew in place of their crests of hammered gold, and hunters forgot the hoopoes. As a result they grew in numbers, from hundreds to thousands.

That is why hoopoes have beautiful heads, and why there are so many of them, and why they enjoy living near the dwellings of people.

The Sultan's Bad Breath

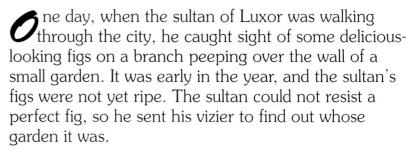

One day, when the sultan of Luxor was walking through the city, he caught sight of some delicious-looking figs on a branch peeping over the wall of a small garden. It was early in the year, and the sultan's figs were not yet ripe. The sultan could not resist a perfect fig, so he sent his vizier to find out whose garden it was.

The vizier soon returned and told the sultan that the garden belonged to a poor merchant. 'I have told the merchant,' the vizier said, 'that you, the sultan, wish to pay him the high honour of accepting one of his figs at your daily audience tomorrow.'

Each day the sultan sat in the first courtyard of his palace and listened to the requests and complaints of his people and accepted their gifts. At dawn the next day the merchant came to the sultan's audience with a beautiful fig on a plate. It was turning a gorgeous purple and just starting to soften. An irresistible fig.

The merchant knelt in front of the sultan, saying that it pleased the gods to send him beautiful figs early in the year, and he would be honoured beyond understanding if the sultan would deign to partake of one. 'Or even of a part of one,' he added without thinking.

The sultan nodded slowly. He thought it would be unseemly and un-sultanlike to look too eager to begin. 'I observed the figs on my walk, on a branch peeping shyly over your wall. A sultan should recognize the

40

skills of his people and be willing to accept their gifts. I agree to receive your early fig.'

The merchant bowed low, and came forward with the plate. The sultan lifted the fig by its stem and, tipping his head back and closing his eyes in sheer pleasure, drained it empty.

'Mmmmmmm . . . A pharaoh of a fig! A magic carpet of a fig! Do you by chance have . . . er . . . any . . . er . . . more?'

Of course the merchant had some more, though he was hoping to sell them at a good price, not give them all away to his sultan. The sultan must have noticed the merchant hesitate, because he said, 'Of course, there will be a reward for bringing such amazing figs to your sultan before the season for figs is here. Vizier, bring my writing brush.' And the sultan wrote out an order for gifts to be delivered to the merchant's house the same afternoon.

The merchant went back home and waited. Late in the afternoon the vizier arrived. He brought money, fruit, cooked pigeons and a donkey. The merchant gaped. He could hardly believe his luck. As the vizier left he looked rather sternly at the merchant, and said that of course in return for the reward the sultan would be expecting another fig of the same high standard on the following day.

This happened every day while the figs lasted. The sultan satisfied his passion, and the merchant accumulated gifts of rich carpets, camels, silver and gold ornaments, land, ebony couches and chairs, and goodness knows what else. In fact the sultan gave the merchant so much that the vizier, who looked after the treasure and riches of the country, began to think that the sultan would end up giving it all away. He grew angry and jealous. He also disapproved of gifts going to a poor merchant – except that the merchant was not poor any longer; he was wealthier than the vizier, which made it even worse.

The vizier devised a plan to put an end to the farce of the fig. He went round to the merchant's house and said, 'The sultan is pleased to receive your figs, and wishes to keep your friendship. He is even considering offering you to his daughter in marriage. There is one

problem, though. And that is the garlic. You will not mind him saying so, he says, but the stench of garlic on your breath is like the stink of a large farmyard. Can you, he asks, do anything about it? The sultan finds it very difficult not to insult you by backing away or throwing his cloak over his face. He suggests that tomorrow when you visit him you tie a shawl round your head.'

And off he went.

The merchant was shocked to think he'd breathed garlic into the sultan's face. He breathed into his hand and smelled it to check. It wasn't too bad, he thought, but perhaps that was because it was his own breath he was smelling. Anyway, it was easy to put a shawl round his head and cover his mouth, and the next day he went to the sultan well wrapped up.

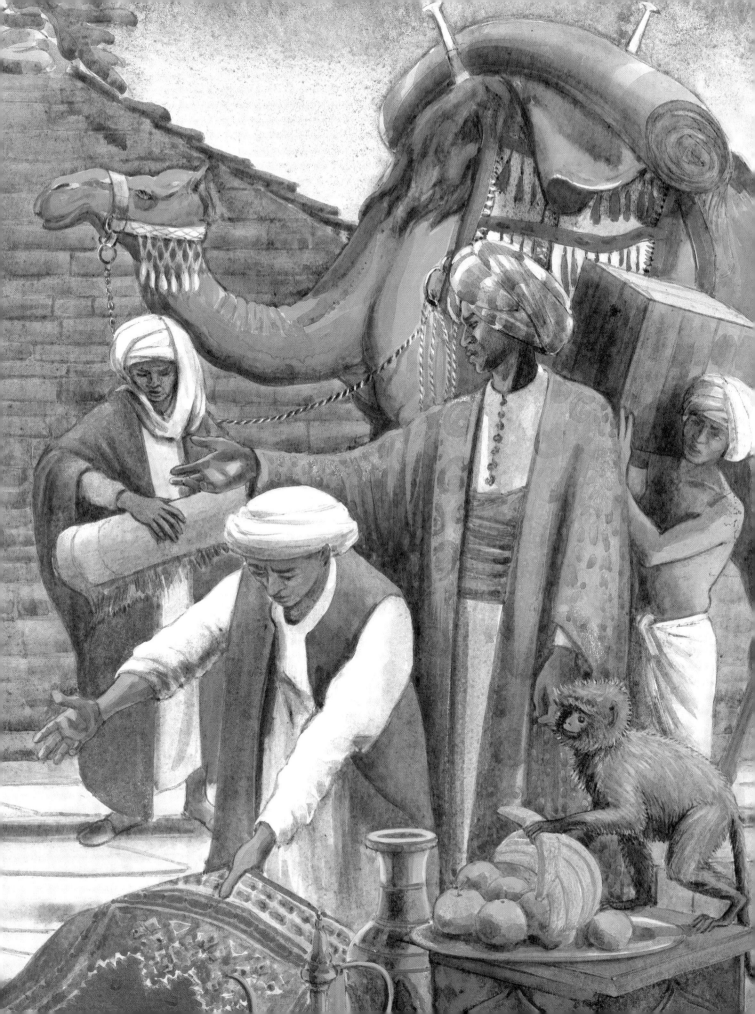

The sultan, of course, was not expecting the merchant to arrive dressed in this unusual fashion. He couldn't think what was going on. But out of politeness he held his audience without mentioning the shawl round the merchant's head. However, after the audience, the sultan asked the vizier what was the meaning of the merchant coming with his face wrapped in a shawl. The vizier said he really didn't know, but that he would find out immediately. And off he went, pretending to be on his way to the merchant.

The vizier went round the corner to a coffee shop, and waited long enough to have gone to the merchant's and back. Then he returned to the sultan, pretending to know what was wrong. 'My lord, let me tell you what the merchant says, in his own words. He says that he is honoured beyond understanding by your gifts and your friendship, but there is a problem. You will not mind him saying so, he says, but the stench of your breath is overwhelming, and unexpected, coming as it does from a sultan. He says it is more like the smell that comes from a farmyard, and hopes you will forgive him for covering his face. He says that otherwise he might faint in your presence.'

'That's what he says, is it?' the sultan said. 'I see.' He fell silent. The vizier was waiting for the sultan's fury to break, but it did not. Instead, he smiled. 'It is good to know the truth,' he said, 'and it is good to know that my subjects do not go in fear of me. I shall see the merchant tomorrow and reward him for his honesty.'

The vizier could only think that his clever plan had gone badly wrong, and he was not sure what to do.

The next day the merchant arrived as usual, and spoke for a few minutes with the sultan. At the end of the audience, the sultan gave him a note, which he sealed. 'Now go to the treasury,' he said, 'and you will be well rewarded for your honesty in the matter of the breath.'

The vizier saw and heard all this, and being by now even more jealous of the favour shown to the merchant, he decided that he himself, the vizier, should take the merchant's place and receive the latest gift from the sultan.

He thought of a trick to take the merchant's place and carry his note to the treasurer. 'I have to go to the treasury each morning, sir. If you wish, I can take your note with me. I happen to know that it is a command to the treasury to give you a thousand pieces of gold. I can collect your gift and deliver it this afternoon, on my rounds through the city.'

This sounded fine to the merchant, and he agreed.

Off went the vizier to the treasury. He handed the sealed note to the treasurer, and stood back, waiting for his gift to be counted. As he waited, the treasurer unsealed the note and read it. He looked surprised, then turned to whisper to two of the guards. They came across to the vizier, and took a firm grip on each arm.

'What is this? What are you doing?' The vizier protested and struggled, but before he knew what was happening, the two guards had forced him to kneel and had chopped his head off.

Later, at the audience, the sultan couldn't believe his eyes when he saw the merchant come in, with his head wrapped up as usual. He turned to ask the vizier what on earth was happening, but of course the vizier hadn't been able to come. Instead, the treasurer arrived, carrying a bag. 'I have carried out your orders, my lord,' he said, going across to the sultan and gesturing to the bag.

The sultan looked puzzled, and peered in, then stepped back with a horrified cry. 'What have you done? Did I not tell you to behead the bearer of the note?'

'Yes, my lord, that is what we did. The vizier brought us a signed note instructing the treasurer to order his guards to strike off the bearer's head. The vizier was the bearer, the bearer's head is in the bag.'

The sultan didn't understand. He asked the merchant for his help in explaining the mystery. 'Why is the vizier dead and not you? You have insulted me in the matter of the shawl, and escaped punishment. I cannot pardon you.'

The merchant was astonished. 'Insulted *you* in the matter of the shawl, my lord? The vizier ordered me to wear it.'

And so the truth came out. The sultan was at first angry, then amused. 'Well then, the vizier wanted to take your place, and he has succeeded in doing so. I am now one vizier short. Would you like to take his place?'

'Why not?' said the merchant immediately.

'And perhaps marry my daughter?'

'Why not?' he said, even quicker.

'A fig for being a poor merchant,' he thought.

Notes

Atum (say Ah'-tum) (p. 6-13)
Sun god, the first being and the creator of the world. In some stories he rose out of the black waters of Nun, hidden in the First Lotus.

Byblos (say Bib'-lus) (p. 15, 18-19, 21)
A city on the coast of Lebanon.

Djinns (say jins) (p. 36)
Invisible creatures made of smokeless fire. They perform physical labours, like pulling the magic carpet of Solomon.

Geb (p. 8-11, 13)
Earth god, the son of Shu, the air, and Tefnut, moisture.

Horus (say Haw'-rus) (p. 18-19, 21-22)
The son of Isis. He had to be hidden in the reeds to escape the murderous rage of Seth.

Isis (say Eye'-sis) (p. 12-13, 18-22, 29)
Goddess of magic, and the wife of Osiris.

Ka (say Kar) (p. 24-25, 30)
A kind of soul. It is like the ghostly double of a person and travels about on its own. A person's Ka is visible.

Memphis (say Mem'-fis) (p. 4, 23, 30, 33, 35-37)
The capital city of ancient Egypt.

Mummies (p. 30)
Dried and preserved bodies, wrapped in layers of cloth. Animals were mummified as well as people.

Nun (say Noon) (p. 6, 8, 10-13)
The black, motionless waters that existed before life came to the world. Nun surrounds the world, and always threatens to break back into it and wash it away.

Nut (say Noot) (p. 8-12)
The sky, the wife of Geb. In the creation story she is pushed high above Geb by Shu, and so separated from the earth.

Osiris (say Oh-sy'-ris) (p. 5, 12-22)
The son of Nut, and the most important Egyptian god. Osiris lives again when the Nile rises and crops grow.

Papyrus (say Pap-eye'-rus) (p. 4, 23, 34)
A kind of paper used for writing on. It was made from wide strips of reed laid across each other in two or three layers. They were soaked then dried.

Pharaoh (say Fare'-oh) (p. 5, 23, 41)
The Egyptian name for a king.

Ptah (say P-tah) (p. 4, 23-24, 33)
God of creation in some stories. Things are made when he pronounces their names.

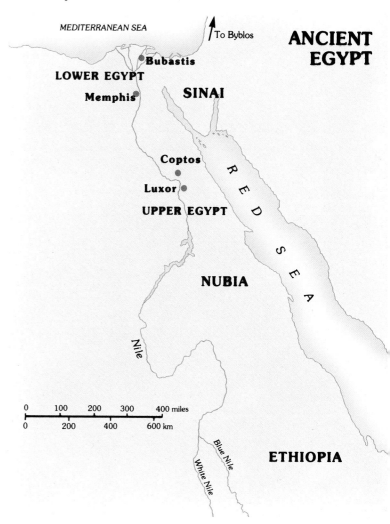

Scribes (p. 23)
Professional readers and writers. They were trained to read and write from an early age until they were about sixteen.

Scrolls (p. 23, 29, 31)
Egyptian books. Sheets of papyrus were joined together and rolled up.

Seth (p. 5, 12-13, 15, 20-21, 23)
God of chaos and darkness. He is associated with storms and the searing hot winds from the desert.

Shu (say Shoo) (p. 8-11)
The first son of Atum, and god of air. He is shown in pictures with raised arms.

Tefnut (say Tef'-noot) (p. 8, 10)
The first daughter of Atum, and goddess of moisture.

Thoth (p. 12, 14, 23-25, 28-31, 33, 35)
God of wisdom. He records all the knowledge of the world in his book, the Book of Thoth. He is the protector of learning.

Viziers (p. 40-46)
The Pharaohs' chief ministers.

Writing brush (p. 34, 41)
A kind of brush used before pens were invented, for drawing hieroglyphs on papyrus, pottery or bits of limestone.

Further Reading

Egyptian Legends and Stories, M V Seton-Williams (Rubicon Press, 1988)

Gods and Pharaohs from Egyptian Mythology, Geraldine Harris (Peter Lowe, 1982)

Tales of Ancient Egypt, Roger Lancelyn Green (Penguin/Puffin, 1967)